CLAYDON
WAS A
CLINGY CHILD

Cressida
Cowell

Hodder
Children's
Books

A division of Hodder Headline Limited

Claydon was a clingy child.

He would not let go of his mother's leg.

'It's safer here,' said Claydon.

CLAYDON WAS A CLINGY CHILD

by Cressida Cowell

British Library Cataloguing in Publication Data
A catalogue record of this book is available from
the British Library.
ISBN 0 340 75723 X (HB)
ISBN 0 340 75724 8 (PB)

Copyright © Cressida Cowell 2001

The right of Cressida Cowell to be identified as
the author and illustrator of this Work has been asserted
by her in accordance with the Copyright, Designs and
Patents Act 1988.

This paperback edition published 2002
10 9 8 7 6 5 4 3 2 1

Published by Hodder Children's Books
a division of Hodder Headline Limited
338 Euston Road London NW1 3BH

Printed in Hong Kong

So wherever Mummy went...

...Claydon went too.

When Mummy went skateboarding...

...Claydon went too.

When Mummy played rugby,
Claydon went too.
'It's safer here,' said Claydon.

Claydon's bear did
not agree.

'Claydon,' he said, as he was dragged
through the mud…

'…there comes a time,' he said,
as he flew through the air…

'...when it might be best for us to
let go of your mother's leg.'

'Your mother,' he said, as he was
sat on by somebody large ...

'... while a fine woman, is fond of the More Dangerous Forms of Exercise.'

When Mummy
went skydiving,

Claydon went too.

'It's safer here,' said Claydon.

'Safer in what way exactly?'
asked Claydon's bear.

'Your mother,' he said,
as they rushed towards
the ground at a hundred
miles an hour…

When Mummy went bicycling,
Claydon went too.

'It's safer here,' said Claydon.

'Claydon,' said Claydon's bear, 'the time has definitely come to let go of your mother's leg. We are going round and round...'

'May I point out,' he said, as they whizzed past Claydon's own blue tricycle, 'that we could ride that on our own – rather quietly.'

Claydon looked at his own blue tricycle.

It was blue.

It was beautiful.

He could ride it

on his own

rather quietly

if only he could...

...Let go!

'Goodness Gracious!'
said Claydon's mummy.

'**Toot, toot,**'
said Claydon.
'It's safer here,'
said Claydon's bear.

And everywhere that Claydon went...

...the tricycle went too.

And he always rode it rather quietly.
Until one day...